Reginald Hill

Reginald Hill is a native of Cumbria and a former resident of Yorkshire, the setting for his outstanding crime novels, featuring Dalziel and Pascoe, 'the best detective duo on the scene bar none' (*Daily Telegraph*). His writing career began with the publication of *A Clubbable Woman* (1970), which introduced Chief Superintendent Andy Dalziel and DS Peter Pascoe. Their subsequent appearances have confirmed Hill's position as 'the best living male crime writer in the English-speaking world' (*Independent*) and won numerous awards, including the Crime Writers' Association Cartier Diamond Dagger for his lifetime contribution to the genre.

The Dalziel and Pascoe novels have now been adapted into a hugely successful BBC television series, starring Warren Clarke and Colin Buchanan.

Visit www.AuthorTracker.co.uk for exclusive information on Reginald Hill

By the same author

Dalziel and Pascoe novels

A CLUBBABLE WOMAN
AN ADVANCEMENT OF LEARNING
RULING PASSION
AN APRIL SHROUD
A PINCH OF SNUFF
A KILLING KINDNESS
DEADHEADS
EXIT LINES
CHILD'S PLAY
UNDER WORLD
BONES AND SILENCE
ONE SMALL STEP
RECALLED TO LIFE
PICTURES OF PERFECTION
ASKING FOR THE MOON
THE WOOD BEYOND
ON BEULAH HEIGHT
ARMS AND THE WOMEN
DIALOGUES OF THE DEAD
DEATH'S JEST-BOOK
GOOD MORNING, MIDNIGHT
THE DEATH OF DALZIEL

Joe Sixsmith novels

BLOOD SYMPATHY
BORN GUILTY
KILLING THE LAWYERS
SINGING THE SADNESS

FELL OF DARK
THE LONG KILL
DEATH OF A DORMOUSE
DREAM OF DARKNESS
THE ONLY GAME

THE STRANGER HOUSE

REGINALD HILL

THE LAST NATIONAL SERVICE MAN

A Dalziel and Pascoe novella

HARPER

Harper
An imprint of HarperCollins*Publishers*
77-85 Fulham Palace Road,
Hammersmith, London W6 8JB

www.harpercollins.co.uk

This paperback edition 2007

First published in Great Britain as part of the anthology
Asking for the Moon
by HarperCollins*Publishers* 1994

Copyright © Reginald Hill 1994

Reginald Hill asserts the moral right to
be identified as the author of this work

A catalogue record for this book is
available from the British Library

ISBN-13: 978-0-00-651017-8
ISBN-10: 0-00-651017-5

Typeset in Meridien by Palimpsest Book Production Limited,
Grangemouth, Stirlingshire

Printed and bound in Great Britain by
Clays Ltd, St Ives plc

TO YOU

DEAR READERS

without whom the writing would be in vain
and
TO YOU

STILL DEARER PURCHASERS

without whom the eating would be infrequent

THIS BOOK IS DEDICATED

in
appreciation
of
your loyalty

in
anticipation
of
your longevity

in admiration
of
your taste

NON SCRIBIT, CUIUS CARMINA NEMO
LEGIT

Introduction

Writers create futures; pasts create themselves.

I had been chronicling the adventures of Dalziel and Pascoe for a quarter of a century before my thoughts turned to their very first encounter. At various points in the series reference had already been made, sometimes fleetingly, sometimes in detail, to their backgrounds and origins, but 'til 1994 their earliest appearance as a duo had been in the very first book, *A Clubbable Woman*, with Fat Andy the detective superintendent in charge of Mid-Yorkshire CID and Peter Pascoe his sergeant.

Some dozen books later, their relationship had developed and deepened and much fine detail had been recorded, so when I started researching their first meeting, I was far from a free agent.

It couldn't, for instance, be love at first sight!

Over the years Dalziel's attitude to graduate entry to the police service may have moderated a little. In fact, he has been heard to agree that it might be possible to make something of a college boy - *if you catch the bugger young!* But back then he would have been in full anti-intellectual spate.

This raised the question, why on earth would he, the Fat Controller, have allowed someone like Pascoe to be wished upon him?

The truth was obvious. Because of course when Pascoe arrived in Mid-Yorkshire, Dalziel wasn't yet in charge of CID, merely a Chief Inspector with a boss he refers to as Zombie.

And why would Detective Constable Pascoe have transferred from the midlands to Mid-Yorkshire?

Ironically, to escape from a fascist superintendent with a halitosic daughter who fancies him!

It was all perfectly clear. Now all I had to do was find a dramatic vehicle for their first trip out together. Almost immediately one came nosing into view.

Back in the Spring of time when I was a lightfoot lad doing National Service, the only trouble to my dreams wasn't the threat that the Red Army might one day come pouring over the nearby East German border. No, it was the fear that accident or alcohol might lead me beyond one of the many minor misdemeanours necessary for survival in the army into a major offence – a surprisingly easy transition. Not only could this mean incarceration in the dreaded glasshouse but also, as frequently pointed out by various sadistic NCOs, such time did not count towards your two years National Service. Catch-22 still applied in the fifties. The bastards could do anything to you that you couldn't stop them from doing.

Of course, I survived the experience with nothing more troublesome than long bouts of severe boredom, and back in the real world my fear soon dwindled to a pin prick. But long after I came out, long after the conscription legislation was repealed, the thought would pop up in my mind that perhaps, somewhere, some poor sod who never wanted to go into the army in the first place might still be languishing behind bars – the very last National Service man.

To a writer even bad dreams are material. I began to create him in my notebook, not an innocent by any means, but you don't have to be innocent to feel hard done by. No, this was a man who would not merely lie in his cell dreaming revenge, he would have the will and capacity to pursue it!

I had my story. All I had to do was fit Dalziel and Pascoe into it, and they would have their first encounter, sowing the seeds of all that was to grow between them until that day long in the future when they would have their last.

And has it arrived? I hear you ask anxiously.

To discover that, you will need to take one giant leap forward from *The Last National Service Man* to *The Death of Dalziel*.

Happy landing!

Reginald Hill
Cumbria
March 2007

THE LAST NATIONAL SERVICE MAN

'I'm late, I'm late, for a very important date,' sang Detective Constable Peter Pascoe.

In moments of stress his mind still trawled through the movies in search of a proper reaction.

'It's an immature tic you may grow out of when you've had enough Significant Experience of your own,' an irritated girlfriend had once forecast. 'Ring me when it happens.'

He hadn't rung yet. Surely his move to Mid Yorkshire where they sold Significant Experience by the bucketful would work the cure? But a fortnight into his new job, when he woke to discover he'd slept through his alarm, the section house boiler had failed, and there were three buttons missing from his only clean shirt, he'd immediately dropped into a Kenneth Williams panic routine straight out of *Carry on Constable*.

Sod's Law was confirmed when he got to the station. No time to grab a bite in the canteen, of course; hardly time to grab the essential file from the CID room: then the phone had rung just as he was passing through the door. Not another soul in sight, so like a fool, he'd answered it.

It had been some snout urgently requiring the DCI and not about to push something useful towards a mere DC. Five minutes getting that sorted. Then the Riley reluctant to start; every light at red: traffic crawling at sub-perambulator speeds (did they have different limits up here?); one side of every road dug up (water, or burial of the dead – which had finally arrived?).

And now, in the courts' car park, not a space in sight except one marked RECORDER.

Sod it, thought Pascoe. Little high-pitched instrument played by some geezer in a ruff couldn't need all that much room.

He gunned the Riley in, and was out and running up the steps before the Cerberic attendant could bark more than the first syllable of 'Hey-up!'

Why did the natives need this ritual exordium before they communicated? he wondered. Not properly a greeting, a command or even an exclamation, it was entirely redundant in the vocabulary of a civilized man.

He burst through the swing doors, and thought, 'Hey-up!' as he spotted a familiar face. Well, not really familiar. He'd known it for only two weeks and not even a lifetime could make it familiar. But unforgettable certainly. Straight out of Hammer

Films make-up. They'd broken the mould before they made this one, ho ho.

'Sergeant Wield,' he gasped.

'Constable Pascoe,' said Wield. 'Now we've got that out of the way, you're lost.'

'You mean I'm late,' said Pascoe. 'Sorry but—'

'Nay lad. Mr Jorrocks, the magistrate is late, which means you'll not be called for another half-hour. What *you* are is lost. Magistrates' court is in the other wing. This is where the big boys play.'

With that face it was impossible to tell whether you were being bollocked or invited to share a joke. And what was Wield doing here anyway? Checking up? If so he was in the wrong place too . . .

Wield answered the question as if it had been asked.

'Our own big boy's here today,' he said. 'Come back all the way from Wales to give evidence. I need a word.'

'Mr Dalziel, you mean? Oh yes. I heard he was visiting.'

Pascoe knew the name shouldn't be pronounced the way it looked but hadn't quite got the vocalization right. This time, perhaps because of the Welsh connection, it came out as *Dai Zeal*.

Wield's mouth spasmed in what might have been a smile.

'*Dee Ell*,' he said carefully. 'You've not met him yet, have you?'

Detective Constable Pascoe's transfer from South

Midlands to Mid-Yorkshire CID had taken place while Detective Chief Inspector Dalziel was in Wales as part of a team investigating allegations of misconduct against certain senior officers. The Fat Man had been pissed off at being turned into what he called 'a bog-brush'. Wield suspected he was going to be even more enraged to discover that the CID boss, Superintendent 'Zombie' Quinn, had taken advantage of his absence to approve the newcomer's transfer.

Trouble was, Pascoe was everything Dalziel disliked: graduate, well spoken, originating south of Sheffield. Wield still had to make his mind up about the lad, but leastways he shouldn't be tossed to a ravening Dalziel without some warning. Not even a bubonic rat deserved that.

'No, but I've heard about him,' said Pascoe neutrally, unaware that Wield's finely tuned ear was well up to detecting the note of prejudgemental disapproval in his voice.

'Come along and see him in action,' said the sergeant. 'You can spare a few minutes.'

'What's the case?' asked Pascoe as they climbed the stairs.

'Sexual assault,' said Wield. 'DCI was leading a drugs raid. Kicked a door open and found what was allegedly a rape in progress.'

'Allegedly?'

'House was a knocking-shop, woman's got three convictions for tomming. Accused's got Martineau defending him. He hates Mr Dalziel's guts.'

That's a lot of hating, thought Pascoe as he tiptoed into the court and had his first glimpse of the bulky figure wedged in the witness box.

Flesh there was in plenty, but more Sydney Greenstreet than Fatty Arbuckle. This was all-in wrestler running to seed rather than middle-aged guzzler running to flab. And if any notion of the comic book fat man remained, it stopped when you moved up from the body to that great granite head which looked like it could carve its way through pack-ice on a polar expedition.

A lemon-lipped barrister with scarcely enough flesh on him to make one of Dalziel's arms was asking questions in a voice which did not anticipate co-operation or trust. 'So you, Chief Inspector, were the first person through the door?'

'Yes, sir.'

His voice like a ship's cannon booming down a fjord.

'Where you found the defendant and Miss X on the bed, sexually coupled?'

'Yes, sir.'

'Now please think carefully before you answer the next question. Did you *immediately* form the opinion that the defendant was using duress?'

Dalziel thought carefully.

He said, 'No, sir. I did not.'

'Really?' said Martineau, surprise mingling with triumph. 'And why not?'

'Well, I don't expect he had time to put one on, sir.'

When order was restored the judge fixed a stern gaze on Dalziel and said, 'I don't know whether your hearing or your taste is defective, Chief Inspector, but what Mr Martineau wishes to ascertain is whether you *immediately* formed the opinion that sex was taking place against Miss X's will, or was it her subsequent behaviour and allegations which brought up this possibility?'

'Oh aye. I'm with you. It were immediate, m'lud.'

'I see. Perhaps you can explain why.'

'Well, first off, he had his right hand round her throat like he was keeping her quiet by strangling her, and his left hand were holding both her wrists above her head so she couldn't hit him . . .'

Martineau's body and voice shot up together.

'My lord! These assumptions . . .'

'Yes, yes. Mr Dalziel, just describe what you saw without giving us the benefit of your inferences, please.'

'Yes, sir. Sorry. Main thing was, soon as I saw the defendant's face, I said to myself, hello—'

Martineau was now soprano with indignation.

'My lord, witness cannot be allowed to imply—'

'Thank you, Mr Martineau,' interrupted the judge. 'I'm grateful as always for your assistance in points of law, but I'm sure that an officer of Mr Dalziel's standing was not about to say anything contrary to the rules of evidence.'

'Nay, sir!' said Dalziel all injured innocence. 'Tha knows I'd never mention a man's record in court, no matter how rotten it were. All I was going to say was, I said to myself, spotty little scrote like that, I bet he'd have to use force to get his own mother to kiss him goodnight!'

Under cover of the renewed laughter, Wield drew Pascoe out of the court.

'I don't believe it!' exclaimed the younger man as they went back downstairs. 'He's turning the whole thing into music hall. Is he for real.'

'Weren't impressed then?' said Wield.

'Impressed? I was horrified! It's bad enough that poor woman having to go through the trauma of a trial without some insensitive clown playing it for laughs.'

'I did tell you the raid were in a knocking-shop and she's got convictions—'

'And that means she's fair game, does it?' interrupted Pascoe indignantly. 'I thought everyone was entitled to equal protection under the law. Excuse me. I'd better get off to my case.'

Wield watched him stride away. Nice mover, head held high, good shoulders, slim body, long legs. Lead us not into temptation. Not that there was much chance of that, not in the force. They might be marching for gay rights in San Francisco, but here in Mid Yorkshire, gay was still what poets felt when they saw a bunch of head-tossing daffs. There was even a holiday company in the High Street called Gay Days Ltd. Caused a lot of misunderstanding with tourists from the louche south!

Any road, he couldn't see Constable Pascoe being around long enough to break any hearts. Zombie (which was what Dalziel had christened Detective Superintendent Quinn after catching him enjoying a post-prandial snooze in his office) might propose but everyone knew that in the end Fat Andy disposed.

'Penny for 'em,' said Dalziel who despite his bulk could come up on you like Umslopagaas.

'You'd want change, sir,' said Wield. 'Mr Martineau didn't keep you long.'

'Mebbe it was something I said. I saw you ear-wigging. Brought a friend, did you?'

Even under forensic assault the Fat Man didn't miss much.

'DC Pascoe. Transfer from South Midlands. Highly recommended, top promotion grades, good on the ground, graduate entry . . .'

'Wash your mouth out, Wieldy! Christ, moment I turn me back, Zombie's trawling the boneyards for the living dead. Where's he at now?'

'Committal proceedings. His first day, stopped two guys on suss by the auction mart. Found they had some weaners in their pick-up and no proof of ownership.'

'Keen bugger. Sounds straightforward. Let's see what kind of a fist Wonderboy makes of it.'

They found 'Wonderboy' under heavy attack from a sharp little solicitor called 'Bomber' Harris.

'So tell us, Detective Constable, what was your reason for being at the back of the market pens?'

'Just passing, sir.'

'Just passing? Along a cul-de-sac whose only function is that of service road to the remoter storage pens of the auction mart?'

'Well, I'm new to the area and I was finding my way about—'

'So, you were lost. And while in this state of uncertainty, you came upon my clients whose driving aroused your suspicions. How so?'

'They were reversing—'

'Out of a narrow cul-de-sac? Sounds reasonable so far. Go on.'

'They looked as if they wanted to get away very quickly.'

'Ah yes. The famous quick getaway. In reverse. And this made you block their path and examine their truck.'

'Yes, sir. That's when I found the piglets.'

'Weaners I believe is the cant term. How many were there?'

'Eight, sir.'

'You counted them?'

'Well, not exactly. They were quite lively and moving around . . .'

'So how can you be sure there were eight?'

'Because,' said Pascoe with an infant teacher's clarity, 'that was how many Mr Partridge said had been stolen.'

Dalziel groaned and ground his teeth.

Bomber Harris smiled.

'Yes, we have heard Mr Partridge's evidence that

on the day in question he had eight weaners stolen from the auction mart. Also that he has since recovered seven. My clients, who should know, state that they had only six in their pick-up. Why incidentally did you fail to make an accurate count, constable.'

'Well, they got away, sir. The defendants let down the tailboard—'

'At your request? To facilitate your inspection.'

'Yes, sir. And the piglets, the weaners, got out and ran off. But they were recovered later—'

'Really? My clients will be glad to hear it, concerned as they are that their compliance with your instructions should have resulted in such a loss of property.'

'I mean that seven were later rounded up which Mr Partridge identified—'

'You will insist on dragging Mr Partridge into this. There is as yet nothing to prove a connection between the eight which he allegedly lost, the seven which he was fortunate enough to recover, and the six which my clients claim are still missing. As things stand, it seems to me what we have here is a serious allegation of crime unsupported by any *corpus delicti* whatsoever.'

'Perhaps, Mr Harris,' said the magistrate who aspired to judicial wit, 'we should say *corpi* as there were six or seven, or even eight, of them.'

'Indeed, sir. *Corpi*. Very good.'

'*Corpora*,' said Pascoe.

'I'm sorry?' said Harris, histrionically puzzled.

'The plural of *corpus* is *corpora*,' explained Pascoe.

And Bomber Harris smiled and said, 'I'm sure we are both grateful to your classical scholarship, Constable Pascoe.'

'Let's get out of here,' growled Dalziel. 'Before I honk my ring!'

Outside, he said, 'Are we stuck with it, Wieldy, or can we flush the useless turd back down south?'

'Fair do's, sir, he may have settled in by the time you finish in Wales. Still much to do, sir?'

'Too bloody much. It's like the wild bloody west out there. Buggers waiting to ambush you behind every slag heap. Some lovely rugby, but. Going to a match tonight. Only schoolboys, but they've got this fly half who's going to give those tossers down at Twickers a few headaches in the near future, always supposing he survives the GBH his compatriots dish out.'

'Oh good,' said Wield with the false enthusiasm of one who found it hard to understand why society found aggression between men so praiseworthy and affection between men so deplorable. 'Then you'll be heading straight back?'

Dalziel was viewing him with great suspicion.

'You're a bit keen to be shut of me,' he said. 'Come to think of it, what the hell are you doing hanging around here anyway?'

'The Super thought I should have a word, sir.'

'Zombie? What else has the useless sod been doing? Hiring the Dagenham Girls Choir as dog handlers?'

'No, sir. Just worried about you, that's all. He thought you should know that Tankie Trotter's on the loose?'

'Tankie Trotter? You don't mean he's made it at last? Wonders'll never cease.'

'Yes, sir. He were returned to the Wyfies' regimental depot at Leeds for discharge at the weekend. From the sound of it, if he'd been serving a civil sentence, he'd likely have been transferred straight to a nut house. But the army are only too glad to have got rid of him at last.'

'Can't blame 'em. Must be an embarrassment still having a National Service Man on the books after all this time. So why're you telling me this, Wieldy?'

'Seems Tankie had a sort of hate list scratched on his cell wall. Didn't matter how often they made him whitewash it over, it always came back. One name was his old platoon commander's. He's a major now, serving out in Hong Kong. Took his family with him, fortunately.'

'Fortunately?'

'He's got a house out near Burley. It were torched night before last. Empty, thank God. Another name was the RSM when Tankie got called up. He retired last year. He's got a flat in Horsforth. Second floor. Someone picked him out of bed last night and tossed him out of the window. He's in intensive care.'

'And what's all this got to do with me, as if I can't guess,' said Dalziel.

'The third name, in fact the one that was always top of the list, is yours, sir.'

'Well, well,' said Dalziel. 'Nice to know that some folk really mean it when they say they'll never forget. Restores your faith in human nature. So you're the errand boy, are you, Wieldy? Sent to see me safely off the premises so if Tankie trashes me, it won't leave a mess on Zombie's doorstep. You'd think the idle bugger could have shown me enough professional courtesy to come along himself. Then I could have had the pleasure of hitting him over the head with that college kid and getting rid of two useless lumps together!'

'Yes, sir, that would really have shown him the meaning of professional courtesy,' agreed Wield. 'So are you going to go quietly? Seriously, I doubt if Tankie knows where Wales is, and we should have felt his collar by the time you get back.'

'Kind of trail he's leaving, what with flames and folk flying through the air, he shouldn't be difficult to find. You've tried his sister?'

'Yes, I went round to see Judith myself. Only she weren't there. Taking a little break. Touring in the West Country. What do you think, sir?'

'Anyone else I'd have said, wise move,' said Dalziel frowning. 'But them two have got a lot of common baggage to haul, and I don't just mean being twins. Still, things being the way they are, that might be even more reason for her to hide. Any road it's down to you, Wieldy. I'll just get a cup of tea and a wad and I'll be on my way.'

'You'll get better value in a transport caff, sir.'

Dalziel shook his head and said wonderingly, 'You're turning into a right hard bastard, Wieldy. But I'll not hang around where I'm not wanted. See you in a week or two. Cheers.'

That wasn't so hard, thought Wield as he watched the Fat Man head out to the car park. Mebbe he was learning sense at last. Or mebbe he was heading down to the station to throw Zombie out of the window! Still, what a mere sergeant could do, a mere sergeant had done.

He glanced down the long corridor which led to the magistrates' wing. Distantly he saw Peter Pascoe approaching.

'Lost again?' he said when the youngster joined him.

'No, sarge. My car's parked out front.'

'So how'd it go?'

'No problem,' said Pascoe. 'Harris is still droning on, but the beak would have to be brain dead not to commit those two jokers on the evidence. I've left word there's no objection to bail, so no need for me to stay, especially as I'm due at a briefing in ten minutes. See you!'

He was off through the doors at a graceful trot.

Didn't notice me and Fat Andy then, thought Wield. Or perhaps he really didn't think he had a problem. One thing was sure. Bomber Harris would have noticed his exit. Worth keeping an eye on the sly sod. He set off down the corridor.

Pascoe meanwhile, with a quick glance around

to make sure the attendant was nowhere in sight, ran down the steps to the Riley. As he got in he could hear the car in the next bay making a meal of getting started. It was a big Rover, facing outwards so it wasn't till he reversed past it that he became aware of the driver. It was Detective Chief Inspector Dalziel.

There was a man sitting beside him, a big man with a Yul Brynner haircut and a blue chin. This didn't mean he couldn't be the Chief Constable, and as Dalziel had probably spotted him anyway, it seemed politic to stop.

He got out and approached smiling. Dalziel ignored him and tried the engine again. It roared impotently.

He tapped on the driver's window. Dalziel's head turned. His leathery lips formed two inaudible words. If Pascoe had not known it to be impossible, he would have guessed the words to be 'Fuck off'.

He tapped again. The man with the polished head spoke. Dalziel slowly wound down the window. His gaze met Pascoe's with a force that almost straightened him up. And the lips were moving again, still inaudibly but this time unmistakably.

'Fuck off!'

'Sorry, sir,' said Pascoe. 'Just thought you were having a spot of bother . . .'

'He one of yours, Dalziel?' growled the man in the passenger seat.

The DCI's expression seemed to suggest the idea

gave great pain. Piqued by this response, and also encouraged by the passenger's tone in his suspicion that he might be brass, Pascoe said brightly, 'Detective Constable Pascoe, sir.'

'Right. Out! Jildi! Move your fat arse!'

Peter Pascoe had become aware very soon after joining the police that the rules of civilized social intercourse no longer applied. But did Chief Constables really speak to Chief Inspectors like this?

Perhaps he'd made a mistake. In fact as the Fat Man slid out of the car and the bald man followed him via the same door, the pointers to error began to mount up.

No reason perhaps why a Chief Constable should not be fluent in the patois. But surely no Chief Constable would wear khaki trousers, heavy black boots, and a sweat-stained green shirt whose rolled-up sleeves revealed the word MUM tattooed on a brawny forearm, the letters wreathed in roses and all enclosed in a ragged fillet of black?

It occurred to him that he was concentrating so much on the specific gravity of the milk, he was ignoring the trout.

One of the man's outsize hands was gripping the back of Dalziel's jacket while the other was forcing the sawn-off barrel of a shotgun against the Fat Man's spine.

'Try anything and his arse says goodbye to his belly,' snarled the man. 'Back in your car!'

Pascoe looked helplessly at Dalziel and said, 'Sir?'

The Fat Man rolled his eyes and said, 'You got yourself into this, lad. You'll have to find your own way out.'

This was new country for Pascoe, in every sense. Certainly he had no Significant Experience to call on. Lots of movies, but the cop in his situation had always had a bull-horn in his hand and a posse of armed policemen at his back. Hadn't he once read a chapter in a textbook about hostage situations?

He looked from the fat man to the bald. It occurred to him that, going by expression alone, their heads were interchangeable. It also occurred to him that it must have been a very boring textbook and he'd probably gone out for a pint and a curry halfway through that chapter.

He got into the Riley and waited.

The bald man pushed Dalziel into the rear seat and slid in beside him. It was a tight squeeze. The gun barrel must have ploughed a furrow in the Fat Man's flesh as it was dragged round from his spine to his belly.

'Go go go!' commanded the bald man.

Pascoe set the car in motion. Not a soul in sight. Where the hell was that blasted attendant when you wanted him? Or Sergeant Wield? Why hadn't he come out of the courthouse? Probably sitting in there somewhere all comfortable with a pot of tea and a fag.

At the exit he said, 'Which way?'

'Left. And drive steady. We pick up a cop car, they'll be picking up little pieces.'

Cop car? What cop car? thought Pascoe as he drove through the town. More chance of seeing a uniform on a nudist beach. And now Sod's Law which had made his journey to the courts seem like a funeral procession was casually flicking every light to green as he approached and letting the light traffic flow with careless ease.

Except for the occasional direction from the bald man, no one spoke. What had happened to all Dalziel's little jokes? thought Pascoe sneeringly. All right for a courtroom where there was nothing but a woman's reputation to worry over. Stick a shotgun in his gut and the case was altered.

Behind him Andy Dalziel was thinking, why the fuck couldn't it have been Wield who'd come out and heard him hammering his deliberately flooded engine? One glimpse of that shaven head and he'd have been off like a lintie to get the car park sown up tighter than a nun's knickers. Outcome still uncertain, but at least Trotter would have had the alternative spelt out loud and clear. Now they were on their way God knows where to face God knows what, and it could be God knows when before anyone got on their trail, or even knew there was a trail to get on!

He paused, fair minded as ever, to give God a chance to share some of His knowledge. All he got was an echo of his own words to Pascoe . . . you'll have to find your own way out.

So be it. He put all recriminations on the back

burner and turned his mind to the problem in hand.

First things first. Useless wanker this unweaned college kid might be, but he deserved to know the score.

'So tell me, Tankie,' he said conversationally. 'What fettle? They treat you all right in the glasshouse?'

'Belt up, Dalziel!' said Trotter, digging the barrel so far into the belly flesh it almost covered the trigger guard.

'Nay, lad. Tha's got something better in mind for me than splattering my guts all over this nice upholstery. Any road, it's only polite to introduce you properly to Constable Pascoe. He's new round here and likely he's not heard of one of our most famous sons. That right, Pascoe? You've not heard of Tommy Trotter?'

'Sorry, sir. No, I haven't.'

'Thought not. You might have a certificate or whatever it is you get in them colleges, but your education's been sadly neglected. Right, Tankie?'

Trotter said unemotionally, 'You think you can jerk my string, Dalziel, best think again. I've been needled by experts. I cut loose, it's 'cos I want to cut loose.'

'I believe it, Tankie. So, Constable Pascoe, what we have here is Thomas Trotter, known to all his friends as Tankie, mebbe because of the way he's built, mebbe because of the way he drinks, I'm not sure. What I am sure of is, Tankie's a real star. Unique. With a bit of luck, we'll never see his like again. You see, lad, Tankie's The Last National Service Man.'

He voiced the phrase with a tremulous awe which gave it capital letters if not inverted commas.

Trotter snarled, 'Shitface, you trying to be cute? That was a derestriction sign. Speed it up to fifty. Left at the next roundabout.'

Shocked to be thus addressed, and impressed by the speed with which the man had spotted his attempt to draw attention by slow driving on the open road, Pascoe obeyed.

In the rear-view mirror his gaze met Dalziel's. Was there a message in those stony eyes?

Brightly Pascoe said, 'Last National Service Man? I don't understand . . .'

'Aye, you'll be too young. Stopped in 1960 or thereabouts. It meant every bugger were conscripted into the forces for two years.'

'Yes, sir, I know that. And I know that every time there's any trouble with rockers or hippies, the Cheltenham set start baying to bring it back.'

'Aye, bit of backbone, taste of discipline, teach 'em a bit of respect,' said Dalziel.

Might have guessed you'd go along with it, thought Pascoe.

'Load of bollocks, but,' continued Dalziel, almost causing Pascoe to drive onto the verge with surprise. 'Only thing National Service did for most lads was turn 'em bad or drive 'em mad. In some cases, both together, eh, Tankie?'

'Why don't you shut your gob?' suggested Trotter, digging the gun barrel even deeper into the Fat Man's side.

'Nay, lad, I'm just bringing the constable up to date,' protested Dalziel apparently impervious to either the pain or the danger. 'He ought to know it's not your fault. You're just a victim. You see, Pascoe, Tankie and me are old friends. He were one of the last to be called up only he didn't want to go. Not without reason, either, only when the Queen offers you her shilling, she don't pay much heed to reason. And me, well, I got the job of going and picking him up and making sure he were handed over safe and sound to our colleagues in the military. Full-time employment for a while, weren't it, Tankie? Number of times you took off and headed back home! It were regimental punishment at first, which were OK. Then you broke that MP sergeant's nose, and that got you into the glasshouse. Now the thing about glasshouse time, Pascoe, is, it don't count towards your two years' National Service. So if you've got a year left to do when you go down for a year, you'll still have a year to do when you come out. Got me?'

'I think I can just about grasp the concept, sir,' said Pascoe with heavy irony.

Dalziel smiled elephantinely.

'Good. I'll make a note of that, constable,' he said softly. And despite all the more immediate and apparently greater dangers, Pascoe felt a shiver go down his spine.

Dalziel resumed.

'So you can see Tankie's problem. The more he hated the army, the wilder he got. But the wilder he got, the longer he had to serve. And the longer he had to serve, the more he hated the army. Had to laugh, some of the tricks he got up to. Burning down the officers' mess! Chucking a grenade under the CO's caravan on an exercise! But they've not got a great sense of humour, the military brass. And that's how Tankie became the Last National Service Man. Right, Tankie?'

'Wrong, you fat bastard,' said Trotter dispassionately. 'It's you who's going to be the Last National Service Man. Next left. No! That one there, you stupid cunt!'

Pascoe had almost overshot the narrow entry into an overgrown lane, once metalled but now potholed and greened by the irresistible pressure of weeds and grass. Any hope that his sudden braking and turn might have drawn attention was vain. Sod's Law had made sure the road ahead and behind was empty. He bumped down the lane for fifty yards till progress was blocked by a five-barred gate. Assuming not even Tankie Trotter would expect him to crash through it, he brought the Riley to a halt.

'Out and open it,' said Trotter. 'Try anything funny and you'll hear the air hissing out of this bag o' wind.'

Pascoe got out and took a deep breath of air. It tasted good.

Run you stupid sod, Dalziel urged mentally. *Run*! Whatever Trotter's threat, his instinctive reaction would likely be to take a potshot at the fleeing man. And if the gun barrel stopped drilling into his gut for even a second . . .

But the prancing academic prat was opening the gate! And now he was getting back into the car. What the hell did they teach them at these sodding colleges. If they went in for mutual masturbation, they'd likely need diagrams!

They passed through.

'Right. Stop. Out and close it,' growled Trotter.

Second chance! Mebbe the lad weren't as daft as he looked. Mebbe he'd worked out he'd have a better chance of escaping when he was behind the car rather than in front of it. Dalziel tensed himself to grab for the barrel the moment he felt it move away from his gut. But the bugger was now shutting the gate, taking real care like he was worried about breaking the Countryside Code! And as he got back in the car, he said insouciantly, 'Lovely day out there.'

Dalziel closed his eyes in pain. Who the hell does he think he is? Captain fucking Oates?

'Drive on,' ordered Trotter.

As the car moved forward Pascoe said, 'You were telling me about Mr Trotter's career, sir.'

Aye, and I'm looking forward to telling you about yours, lad, thought Dalziel savagely.

He said, 'Not much more to tell. Spent so much time serving time, it soon worked out he were

the only conscript left in Her Majesty's Army.
Last bloody National Service Man. The Wyfies
were almost proud of him!'

'The Wyfies?'

'The West Yorkshire Fusiliers.'

'Good Lord, I think they were the lot my great-
grandfather served in.'

'You one of them army bastards? I might have
known,' snarled Trotter.

'Hold on,' protested Pascoe. 'He got killed in
the Great War, that's all the army connection
I've got.'

'What the hell were he doing in the Wyfies?'
demanded Dalziel accusingly. 'Got lost when he
went to sign on, did he?'

'No, sir, I'm sorry to say he was a Yorkshireman.
But we try to keep it quiet,' retorted Pascoe.

This near blasphemous insubordination momen-
tarily caused Dalziel to forget the shotgun, but as
he leaned forward to administer a just rebuke,
Trotter screwed it in another quarter inch. This
time Dalziel let out a gasp of pain as he subsided.
And as his wrath faded, the thought came into his
mind that probably both the insolence and the
insouciance came from the same source. The boy
was scared out of his tiny mind.

He found the thought quite comforting. Last
thing a man up shit creek needs is a red-blooded
hero willing to use his dick as a paddle.

And Pascoe thought: sitting there like Heck-
mondwyke's answer to Buddha, is he really as

unfazed as he looks? Or is his brain so atrophied, he's simply incapable of appreciating the situation? What the blazes has he done to make this madman hate him so much? One thing's for certain: what-ever it was, this isn't the time to bring it up!

Dalziel said, 'Likely you're wondering, constable, how come after so many years of going steady, me and Tankie finally fell out.'

Oh God, thought Pascoe. Completely brain dead!

'No, sir,' he said brightly. 'I wasn't wondering that.'

'And you call yourself a detective! Motive, lad, that's the key. Once you've got a hold on that, the rest'll not be long in coming, as the bishop said to the actress.'

'Stop here,' said Trotter.

The lane had widened into a small overgrown paddock in front of a cottage which was more Gothic than picturesque. True, round the door there were roses rambling and honeysuckles suckling, but they looked more carnivorous than vegetarian, as if their ambition were to devour the house, which indeed slumped sideways like a stricken deer, only supported by a roofless barn on the left-hand side.

'Blow the horn!' ordered Trotter.

Pascoe blew the horn.

The cottage door opened and a woman came out, rubbing floured hands on a flowered apron. It was a scene so rustically domestic that Pascoe thought: it's a wind-up. Wield and the rest of the CID boys are waiting inside with a birthday cake for Fat Andy. But he didn't really believe it, even before the woman stepped back inside and re-emerged with an under-and-over shotgun in her hands.

'Out,' ordered Trotter. 'Shoot the boy if he tries anything.'

The woman nodded as if she'd been told her guests took sugar in their tea.

'Hello, Jude,' said Dalziel. 'Heard you'd gone off for a trip. Nice place you found. Bet it costs more for a week than a fortnight. This boy you may have to shoot is Detective Constable Pascoe. This here's Judith, Tankie's sister. Twins, would you credit it? She got the beauty, he got the brawn. What happened to the brains, God alone knows, and He's not telling us, is he, Jude?'

A smile touched the woman's lips, acting like a tiny light to reveal the true beauty of her features. But her eyes confirmed her twinship. They were the same unyielding grey discs as her brother's.

She said, 'Some things are beyond working out with brains, Mr Dalziel. You just swim with the tide.'

'Just what I keep telling these folk with degrees,' said Dalziel.

'Inside,' said Tankie.

Pascoe moved in first with the woman in close attendance. Dalziel came behind, the gun barrel still drilling into his spine.

The cottage was almost as decrepit inside as

out, but some effort had been made to render it inhabitable and there was a good smell of baking coming from the kitchen.

'Scones,' said Dalziel expertly. 'I could murder a home-baked scone with fresh butter and some strawberry jam.'

Wish he'd stop harping on about killing, thought Pascoe.

They were herded past the kitchen into a stone-flagged, windowless room which must have been built as a dairy. Whatever the state of the rest of the building, this was solid, constructed of great granite blocks thick enough to keep out any warmth from the sun. It was lit by a solitary bulb dangling from the ceiling. It contained a narrow metal-framed bed covered by a thin flock mattress. By the bed stood a rusting metal locker, open to reveal various items of clothing.

'Inspection in ten minutes,' said Trotter stepping back and slamming the door.

Pascoe grabbed the handle and rattled it like they always did in the movies. But he'd heard the key turn in the lock, and the woodwork looked disturbingly solid.

He turned to find Dalziel had taken his trousers off.

'Sir, what are you doing?' he asked, not certain he wished to know the answer.

'Like Judith said, you just swim with the tide. Even if you're a shark,' said Dalziel, removing his shirt. 'I were telling you how Tankie and me fell out, weren't I? Simple misunderstanding. God, I'd forgotten how this stuff itched!'

He'd taken a khaki shirt from the locker and was putting it on. As he buttoned it up, he continued talking.

'Four years back Tankie were getting close to discharge. Then some silly twat of a sergeant spoke to him insensitively. Naturally Tankie nutted him. Then he helped himself to a Champ and took off home. That's where I found him, waving an axe and demanding to know where his mam and Judith was. I told him his mam had taken badly and was down at the infirmary and I said if he gave me the axe, I'd make sure he got in to see her. He saw sense and gave me the axe and I drove him down the infirmary. Only when he got out of the car, the MPs were waiting for him. He seemed to think it were my fault. I still think I could have sorted things out and got him in to see his mam, only by the time I could make myself heard, Tankie had cracked one bugger's head open, broken another's arm and was marking time on a corporal's goolies. There weren't much scope for reasonable debate after that. They dragged him off, and a couple of hours later, his mam died. Christ, these are a bit tight. Long time since anyone thought I was thinner than I am!'

He'd pulled on a pair of grey denim fatigue trousers and was having difficulty fastening them up. Next he squeezed his feet into one of the two pairs of boots in the bottom of the locker. The laces tied, he now began to lay all the remaining clothes on the bed and folded them into neat geometric shapes. Pascoe recalled seeing Sean Connery do this in *The Hill*.

'You're getting ready for a kit inspection,' he said incredulously. 'This is what Trotter meant when he said *you* were going to be the Last National Service Man.'

'Glad they taught you to think at you kindergarten,' said Dalziel. 'Pity they didn't teach you to think fast.'

'They taught me to think logically,' said Pascoe grimly. 'And logic tells me we should be looking for ways of getting out of here, not wasting time going along with this madman's fantasies.'

'And that's your very best thought, is it?' sneered Dalziel. 'You listen to me, sunshine. Time for you to have great thoughts was back there at the gate when you were out of the car and Tankie were in it. But you missed your chance, and you're in the army now, and you're not paid to think!'

'Now hold on,' said Pascoe. 'Of course I thought of making a run for it back there. But I believed him when he said he would blow you away. What I did manage to do though was drop my wallet with my warrant card in it by the gate. If someone finds it and hands it in . . .'

He hadn't expected fulsome praise for his ingenuity but he was taken aback by Dalziel's expression, as if he'd chewed on a chocolate drop and found it was a sheep dottle.

'All right,' he said defensively. 'At least I tried something which still seems better to me than just going along with Trotter.'

'You reckon?' said Dalziel. 'What do you want me to say? That you're not so green as you're cabbage looking? Consider it said. But you'd be well advised to stop being clever and think of nowt but survival. Your own personal survival.'

'It's kind of you to be so concerned about me, sir,' said Pascoe only half satirically. 'But I get the impression it's you Tankie's really after.'

'Right. And that's why I'll play along with the little game he's got planned. What I don't want is you trying any Boy's Own stuff. Don't lose sleep being grateful. Way I see it is, Tankie's not killed anyone yet. Last thing I want is him finding out how easy it is. Now sit down out of the way and let me get this lot sorted.'

Pascoe squatted on the floor near the door, his back against the wall, and uneasily contemplated his new role as the buffer zone between Dalziel and death.

Suddenly the Fat Man who'd been arranging the items on the bed with a housewifely deftness, snapped to attention, chin high, arms rigid, thumbs pointing straight down the side seams of his trousers. He even managed to hoist part of the bulge of his belly to swell the overhang of his chest.

Pascoe had heard nothing, but now the door flew open sending him scrambling out of its path. Trotter strode in and snapped to a halt inches in front of the Fat Man. He was holding the sawn-off under his arm, like a sergeant major's stick, with his finger on the trigger and the barrel levelled at Dalziel's chest.

But his back was to Pascoe, and for half a second he weighed up the odds of flinging himself onto Trotter's shoulders.

Then he saw the full shotgun barrel sticking through the doorway and met the still, grey eyes of Judith Trotter fixed unblinkingly on his face.

Trotter was speaking in a low impassioned voice.

'You are disgusting,' he breathed. 'You are the most disgusting fucking object it's been my misfortune to see since I joined this man's army. WHAT ARE YOU?'

'Disgusting, sir!' bellowed Dalziel.

'And what's this?' asked Trotter turning his attention to the bed.

'My kit, sir!'

'Kit? This milo heap of rubbish? I've seen cleaner looking gear in a Port Said bazaar. In fact, I've seen cleaner cat crap. And you've actually put it on your bed! You've got to sleep on this bed, soldier. This is unhygienic! UNHYFUCKINGGIENIC!'

He stooped, took the mattress in his left hand and threw it against the wall, spilling all the kit onto the floor.

'That's better. Probably saved your life there, soldier. Now when I come back in here in half an hour's time, I want to see this place looking so neat and fucking tidy you could invite Her

Gracious Majesty the Queen Mother, God bless her, to sit down and take tea with you!'

'Sir!' shouted Dalziel.

Trotter stepped back and glanced down at Pascoe who wondered if he was meant to snap to attention too. Sod that!

'You dropped this,' said Trotter tossing Pascoe's wallet onto the floor.

'Oh yes. Thanks,' said Pascoe, trying to conceal his dismay.

'Photo in there. You in a robe and funny hat.'

'Graduation ceremony. When I got my degree. That means—'

'I know what it fucking means! I could've gone to college!'

Pascoe nodded, aiming at something between *Sorry you missed out* and *It's not all it's cracked up to be*, and trying to hide *And I'm to be Queen of the May!*

'Old girl with you, that your mam?'

'Grandmother.'

'Where's your mam then?'

Over Trotter's shoulder, Dalziel mouthed, 'Dead.'

'Dead,' said Pascoe.

Trotter nodded and said, 'This great-grandfather of yours in the Wyfies, squaddie was he? Or an officer?'

Dalziel's huge lips formed the word, 'Captain.'

Thinking, this could be a mistake, Pascoe said, 'I'm not sure but I think he was a captain.'

'So you've got a degree, and your great-granddad

was an officer, and you've still got to jump when this bag of dogshit says Jump!'

'Life does funny things to you,' said Pascoe.

'Don't I know it. What do you reckon to his boots?'

Pascoe glanced at Dalziel's boots.

'They're OK?' he said.

'OK?' echoed Trotter incredulously.

'Well, a bit dull, maybe.' Something in Trotter's expression showed him he was on the right track and warming to the role he went on, 'In fact I think they're pretty filthy.'

'Pretty filthy,' said Trotter savouring the words. 'Why don't you tell him?'

'Yes. Certainly. Look, you, er, Dalziel' – it came out Dyeel – 'why are your boots so, er, filthy?'

'Don't have any polish,' said the Fat Man. 'Aagh!'

The groan was pumped out of him by a sudden jab of the sawn-off shotgun into his belly causing the landslide of his newly promoted chest.

'What do you do when you're addressed by an officer?' screamed Trotter. 'What do you say?'

'I salute, sir!' shouted Dalziel saluting. 'And I say sir, sir! Please, sir, I don't have any polish, sir!'

'That's better. And you watch it, soldier. I catch you not addressing this officer correctly and you'll start to wish you hadn't been born.' To Pascoe he said, 'This one needs watching, sir. Perhaps you could keep an eye on him make sure he gets to work on them boots.'

'But if he doesn't have any polish . . .' objected Pascoe weakly.

'He can spit, can't he?' said Trotter. 'Ought to be able to. Full of piss and wind, I'm sure he's got some spit to spare. Next inspection in thirty minutes if that suits you, sir.'

'Er yes. Er, fine. Er . . . carry on.'

He had a vague recollection from *The Bridge on the River Kwai* that that's the sort of thing they said. It seemed to work. Trotter crashed in a thunderous salute, span on his heel and marched out. The door closed behind him and the key rattled in the lock.

'Not bad,' said Dalziel, sitting on the bed. 'Though you'll need to work on it a bit.'

'Work on what?' demanded Pascoe.

'Being an officer. You're lucky, lad. He's decided to treat you as a genuine buckshee, not just surplus to requirements. You're on the team, but you'd best play to the rules else you might get dropped, from a great height.'

The Fat Man had taken off his boots and was examining them with pursed lips.

'Candle, a metal spoon and some blacking and I'd have these bright enough to get a kiltie done for indecent exposure.'

Pascoe worked this out, then asked, 'You've been in the army, have you, sir?'

'Aye, I've done the state a bit of service,' said Dalziel, spitting on the boot. He wrapped a huge khaki handkerchief (his own, not part of Trotter's issue) round his index finger and began polishing the toecap in with tiny circular movements.

'And which way did it send you? Mad or bad?' enquired Pascoe.

Dalziel stopped polishing and regarded him almost sympathetically.

'Don't give up, lad,' he said.

'I'm sorry?'

'Only reason a sprog like you reckons he can get cocky with someone like me is you don't hold much hope we're ever going to get out of this. My advice is, until you're dying and I'm dead, stay polite and call me sir. Except when Tankie's around that is. Then I'll call you sir and you can call me what you like, short of vulgar abuse. Vulgar abuse is for warrant officers and NCOs.'

The fat oaf isn't joking, realized Pascoe. Curiously it was almost comforting.

He said, 'What did Trotter mean, he could have gone to university?'

'Now that's a good question. More you know about a man, the more you open up opportunity.'

'For negotiation, you mean?'

'For kicking his bollocks into his brain-pan,' growled Dalziel. 'I've been trying to fill you in on the background ever since you let yourself get dragged into this. One thing you've got to grasp about Tankie is, he's no deadhead. He were a bright lad. Passed eleven plus, went to the grammar, got 'O' levels, and it were right enough, he could've stayed on for his 'A's and mebbe gone to college, but that would've meant going away, leaving his sister and his mam alone wi' his father. Now he were a real bruiser, Thomas. Tankie were named for him, but he'd never answer to Tommie so that's why he got Tankie. He grew into it when he got on in his teens, but he were nowt alongside Thomas. Made me feel like a ballet dancer, he did!'

Pascoe had a brief vision of Dalziel in a tutu. It was like a snip from *Fantasia*.

'Glad to see you can still smile, lad,' said the Fat Man. 'Lose your sense of humour, and what you got left? Your job, maybe. But what's a job to a man wi' a degree?'

'This Thomas, am I right in assuming Tankie didn't get on with him?' said Pascoe.

'Am I right in assuming . . .' mocked Dalziel. 'I bet you're a whizz in an interrogation, lad! Yes, you're bloody right! He were a violent sod were Thomas, and he made no distinction of friend, foe or family.'

'Wasn't anything done about him?' demanded Pascoe indignantly.

'Oh we kept him straight in the pubs and streets,' said Dalziel. 'But in them days, what a man got up to in his own house was his own business, short of breaking bones, and not even then sometimes. There was some as said there was more than just beatings went on when the kids were young.'

'Incest, you mean?' said Pascoe horror-struck. 'And you say nothing was done?'

'You need complaint, you need proof,' said

Dalziel grimly. 'One of these days it's all going to start coming out, things that go on behind closed curtains. My old boss, Wally Tallantire, used to say, "An Englishman's home is his knocking-shop, Andy." That's why the church and the Tories rabbit on about the family. Keeps it under wraps.'

This cold view of society chilled Pascoe to the marrow. He said, 'If you thought something like that was going on . . .'

'I didn't, 'cos apart from a few D and Ds, Thomas didn't really bother us. It weren't till Tankie got his call-up papers the family came to my notice. Came as a shock to Tankie. Everyone knew National Service were coming to an end and the clever buggers were finding six new ways of getting deferred before breakfast every sodding morning. Tankie just said he weren't going. That's when I came in the picture. I arrested him, told him not to be stupid and if he didn't let himself be handed over to the army he'd end up in a civvy jail for the duration, and while you could get home from the army, you didn't get leave from prison – though the way things are going, they'll soon be sending the buggers off to Majorca for a few days in the summer!'

Avoiding the temptation of an excursion into the interesting territory of penal philosophy, Pascoe said, 'Not the best advice you ever gave by the sound of it. Sir.'

'Aye, you're right there,' admitted Dalziel. 'The army took him, and once they'd got him, well, as long as he kept on breaking their rules, they were going to keep locking him up in their prisons.'

'But he gave them cause, didn't he?' said Pascoe, surprised by the sympathetic tone of Dalziel's voice.

'Oh aye. He weren't a tearaway, but he had a talent for violence. Not surprising, if you think about it. Kids learn from the way they're brought up, even if it's the wrong way. He hated his dad for being violent, but that was the only way he ever saw for getting the things you wanted from life.'

Pascoe knew sociologists who'd needed a whole lecture to make much the same point. Get Dalziel on campus and maybe they could have got through the degree course in a fortnight! Mind you, he doubted if they made mortarboards to fit heads like that.

'You keep on grinning, your face'll stay like that,' said Dalziel warningly. 'People may stop asking you to funerals.'

All the time he talked, his forefinger kept up its tiny circles on the toe of the boot. Occasionally he examined his progress and administered further salivary unction.

'Did Tankie try to stand up to his father, then?' asked Pascoe.

'Oh aye. But it were no contest. Might be different now he's broadened out and learnt a few dirty tricks. But back then, it took me all my strength to sort the bugger out.'

'You had a fight with him?' cried Pascoe.

'Aye, well, after the first couple of times Tankie bunked off from the barracks and headed home, I started getting some idea of the lie of the land. So I thought mebbe I could set the lad's mind at rest by having a quiet word with Thomas. By God. I'd not want many quiet words like that!'

'What happened?'

'I didn't want to talk in public – this were unofficial, fewer folk who saw us the better. So I waited for him in the ginnel that runs from back of their house to the main road. I spoke him fair. I said, "Thomas, tha's got to stop beating thy wife. If tha wants exercise, there's plenty nearer thy own weight as'll be only too pleased to give it thee." And he said, "Name one." And I hit him.'

Puzzled by this apparent *non sequitur*, or perhaps even *ignoratio elenchi*, Pascoe said, 'You hit him? Why?'

'I reckoned if I'd said, "Me for one," he'd have hit me. So it seemed daft to waste time on the courtesies. Big mistake I made was giving him a fair blow on the chin. It knocked him back but it was a long way off knocking him out. Well, after that, he kicked me to one end of the ginnel and I kicked him all the way back. In the end it settled nowt. Don't know if thumping ever does, but you certainly don't get a man to see things your way by fighting a draw with him.'

Pascoe thought, John Wayne did in *The Quiet Man*, but this is the real Wild West up here.

He said, 'If you were going to these extremes to

try and help Tankie's family, how come he hates you so much he's threatening to kill you?'

'I never told Tankie owt o' this!' said Dalziel indignantly. 'I weren't doing it to make some doolally kid love me. I just wanted to stop the stupid sod giving me grief by heading back here every two minutes. Also Thomas were overdue a good kicking. Like I say, a lot of good it did. Thomas still ruled his house like Godzilla on a bad day. And Tankie kept on heading for home and walking right over any poor sod who got in his way. My fault for being polite.'

Oh God, thought Pascoe. What have I done coming to this dreadful place? And if I get out of here, can it be undone? All the lies he'd told when he applied for transfer, could they be untold? Or would he have to think of a whole new set in order to move onward? Carry on like this and he'd end up on Orkney!

Dalziel was putting his boots on. Finished, he started restoring all the kit which Trotter had strewn over the floor to the bed.

'Best get yourself ready,' advised the Fat Man. 'Tankie said thirty minutes and that's what it'll be.'

'But what do I do?' appealed Pascoe desperately.

'Let's see,' said Dalziel eyeing him speculatively. 'There's all kinds of officers. Brisk efficient adjutant . . . mebbe not . . . Grizzled old warhorse . . . definitely not! Languid . . . aye, that's it. Languid and a bit poncey . . . has trouble wi' his "r"s, calls other ranks other wanks, and probably means it. That's you, lad. Call him Mr Trotter like he was an RSM and treat me like I don't exist. Stand by, he's here.'

His ears were definitely sharper than Pascoe's who once again had to move smartly out of the way of the door.

'Prisoner, 'SHUN!' screamed Trotter.

Dalziel snapped to attention.

'You horrid idle man! You paraplegic or what? Stan' atease! 'SHUN! Stan' atease! 'SHUN!'

Trotter enjoyed himself making Dalziel move from one position to another till the sweat beaded his huge brow. Pascoe didn't much mind the sight till it occurred to him that Dalziel dead of a heart attack might not bode well for his own future. He had a vision of himself digging a grave under the close supervision of the Trotter twins, and when he'd finally excavated a hole large enough for that gross body, hearing the instruction, 'Keep digging.'

He said as languidly as he could manage, 'Ready when you are, Mr Trotter.'

Trotter's head came round and those mad grey eyes focused on this intruder. For a second Pascoe thought the game was over and the man had decided he was after all merely surplus to requirements rather than a genuine buckshee, whatever that was.

Then Trotter stiffened, threw up a salute and said, 'Sir! Prisoner ready for inspection, sir!'

Slowly Pascoe advanced and with an expression of distaste not difficult to simulate he ran his eyes over the Fat Man's frame. Now what was it officers said as they went round the cookhouse? Oh yes.

'Any complaints, my man?'

Who was it who, asked the same question shortly after call-up in 1940, replied, 'Not one in the world, darling. Everything's perfectly ducky'? He couldn't recall. He doubted if the Fat Man was about to make the same answer.

'Nosir!' bellowed Dalziel.

Pascoe found that, despite the underlying menace of the situation, he quite enjoyed this new relationship. He said, 'Good. Mr Trotter, has this man been shown the right way to lay out his kit or have regulations changed to permit a certain amount of idiosyncratic choice?'

Trotter said, 'No, sir. Regulations same as always. You hear what the officer says, you horrible little man?'

He stooped, picked up the mattress and shook the kit to the floor again.

'Next time get it right or you'll wish you had never been born!'

He wheeled towards Pascoe and said, 'Next inspection in twenty minutes, sir?'

The intervals were getting shorter. Must be something he could do to slow the trend. What would happen if he simply used his putative authority to say, no, make it an hour?

He looked into the mad grey eyes and thought,

to hell with that! He'd probably cashier me. With his shotgun!

He looked away and saw the Fat Man's lips forming a word. F . . . something. He wasn't swearing at him again surely! No. It was *food*.

He said, 'Carry on, Mr Trotter.'

It was almost a pleasure to see the expression of fury which passed over Dalziel's face like the shadow of a storm cloud over a fell.

He got the thunderous 'SIR!' and the big salute from Trotter, then just as the man reached the door, Pascoe said, 'Oh, by the way. Has the prisoner had any refreshment?'

Trotter came to a halt at the door and turned. It wasn't a military turn and the look he was giving Pascoe wasn't a military look.

Oh hell, I've bounced him out of character, thought Pascoe.

Trying not to let his languid drawl accelerate into a terrified babble, he said, 'Regulations, Mr Trotter. Everything must proceed strictly according to regulations, or where are we, eh?'

Dead, he thought. That's where. Maybe this was the time for the last despairing leap. Hope that one or both of the shotguns jammed. Did shotguns jam? Probably not. All right, hope that the first wound wasn't totally incapacitating. The adrenalin of fury, or hate, or love, could keep a man going even when full of lead. Like Bill Holden in *The Wild Bunch*. Or Gary Cooper at the end of *For Whom the Bell Tolls*. No. Cancel those. They both snuffed it. Think of Shane riding off into the mountains after the big shoot-out, despite having taken one in whatever part of his apparently anaesthetized anatomy he took it in!

He tensed his muscles. All his life should be passing before him now . . . wouldn't take long . . . barely enough of it for a loony 'toon, let alone a full seven reeler.

Trotter too was stiffening up, slowly resuming his military erectness.

He said, 'Yes, sir. You're right, sir. I'll see to it at once. Sir.'

Then he was gone and the door was locked behind him.

Pascoe sat abruptly on the bed. He realized his legs were gently trembling.

Dalziel said, 'Not bad, lad. Do a bit of acting at this college of thine?'

'No,' said Pascoe. 'I was always more interested in films than the theatre. I once auditioned for a part in *An Inspector Calls* but that was only because there was this girl helping with the production . . .'

Relief was making him garrulous. Dalziel was grinning.

'They didn't put bromide in your tea then?' he said. '*An Inspector Calls*, tha says? Good play that. It were written by a Yorkshireman, did you know that?'

'Yes, surprisingly, I did know that,' said Pascoe.

'I'm glad to hear it. And there's a bit of Yorkshire

in you too, is there, with this great-granddad of yours in the Wyfies? That why you transferred up here?'

Pascoe thought, shall I tell him that I have no interest whatsoever in my great-grandfather and that my sole reason for applying for transfer was to get away from a fascist superior whose methods and morality I equally deplored (but whom I am now starting to recall with nostalgic fondness) and whose halitosic daughter fancied me rotten?

He said, 'A man likes to be near his roots, sir.'

Their gazes locked, the younger man's warm with sincerity, the older man's steadfast with understanding.

Then Dalziel said, 'Bollocks. It'll either be trouble with a tart or your boss. Now give us a hand picking up this lot. What the hell were you playing at? All that idiosyncratic crap, encouraging him to fire it on the floor again?'

'I thought, sir,' said Pascoe stooping to pick up the scattered kit, 'that as he was certainly going to do it anyway, I might as well use the certainty to authenticate my own role.'

'By God, lad, if tha thinks as long-winded as tha speaks, I'm surprised you ever got out of nappies. Glad you picked me up on the food, but. I bet the bugger has me doubling to the cookhouse to collect it.'

'Is that why you suggested it, sir? To get a look around, perhaps suss out a way to escape?' asked Pascoe, impressed.

'Don't be bloody daft,' said Dalziel. 'I suggested it 'cos I'm bloody starving!'

I believe he means it! thought Pascoe helplessly. He's just like all of his type and generation. Not without a certain animal cunning and sharpness, but like an animal, incapable of dealing with more than the immediate moment, the short-term crisis. Either something will turn up or it will go away, that's his philosophy. If we're going to get out of this, it's going to need me to take the initiative.

He said, 'I was thinking, sir. The woman, Judith, how far do you think she'll go with her brother's schemes? I wondered if I should try to work on her . . .'

'Show her your dick, you mean, and tell her you love her? She'd shoot it off without a second thought. Very moral lass, Jude. Very faithful. A one man woman and she'll go all the way to protect them as she's given her loyalty to. Man who gets a lass like Jude can count himself lucky.'

Pascoe had finished collecting the kit, and now he watched as Dalziel once more neatly folded it and arranged it on the bed.

He said, 'Do you really think playing this crazy game is going to get us anywhere?'

'Game? Aye, that's what it is, I suppose. That's what the army is, in peacetime any road, and especially in the glasshouse. None of this daft rehabilitation stuff there. They don't want to make good citizens out of you. They want to make good soldiers, and a good soldier is one who does what he's told, no questions asked.'

'So why's Trotter doing this to you?'

'Because it's the worst thing he can think of. Also because he went through it for years and the poor sod reckons he came out on top. And he thinks a few days of what he suffered for years will break me like a pencil point. Which reminds me.'

He stepped onto the bed which groaned under his weight, removed his belt and with the buckle scratched on the damp granite wall the name TROTTER.

'There,' he said stepping down. 'My name kept Tankie going. Let's see if his can do the same for me.'

'He must have been really fixated on his mother to hate you so much,' said Pascoe.

'Oh aye. There were another reason, but his mum would've been enough. Worshipped her like she was the Virgin Mary. Mebbe that's why he's so bent on getting himself crucified. You'll have noticed the tattoo on Tankie's arm? Got that done when he were a lad. But the black border round it he did himself after she snuffed it. Used boot blacking and a sharpened bed spring while he were in the glasshouse. They thought they might have to cut off the arm, but he survived. Then while he were convalescing, he hit his guard with his drip, stole his clothes, jumped out of a third-storey window and headed home. Only this time it were my home he headed for. My missus opened the door and Tankie just walked in.'

'My God, that must have been a terrible shock for your wife!'

'Aye, might have killed a weaker woman,' said Dalziel with a faint note of regret. 'But once she realized it were me he'd come to kill, they got on like a house on fire. They were sitting having a cup of tea when I walked in. Luckily I'd had some bother with the car and took the bus home, so he had no warning. He jumped up and spilt his tea over his lap. Must've been hot 'cos he didn't half yell! Then I hit him with the teapot and he stopped yelling.'

'And your wife . . . ?'

'She started yelling. It were her Crown Derby pot. I said, serve you right for getting the best china out for a nutter like Tankie, but she didn't see it like that. Why the hell am I telling you all this, Pascoe?'

He turned a coldly speculative gaze on the young DC like a man looking for the watermark in a suspect pound note.

Memo to self, thought Pascoe. This is not a man the details of whose domestic life you want to know.

He said, 'You mentioned another reason Trotter has for hating you.'

'Did I? Not important.'

'Shouldn't I be the judge of that?' insisted Pascoe.

'You keep telling me it's my balls on the block too.'

This sudden descent into the demotic clearly impressed the Fat Man more than any amount of epagogic argument.

He said, 'Mebbe you're right. It's to do with Thomas, Tankie's dad. He died just at the time his mum took ill. I reckon he gave her a punch too many, bust something in her gut. She'd never blow the whistle on him, but he got his come-uppance all the same. Fell into the canal one night coming home pissed. Drowned. Tankie got compassionate for the funeral. Manacled to an MP, naturally. I weren't there, but I heard he spat into the grave.'

'He wasn't on the loose when his father drowned then?'

'Good thinking. No, safely banged up. Inquest brought in accidental death.'

There was an absence of finality in his tone.

Pascoe said, 'You don't think it might have been . . . Judith?'

'You're not just a pretty face then?' said Dalziel. 'Aye, it did cross my mind. But I said, what the hell? No way I could prove it, no way I wanted to prove it!'

'So why should this bother Trotter?'

''Cos I told him I *could* prove it,' said Dalziel gloomily. 'I got to thinking, I didn't much fancy having to look over my shoulder for evermore in case Tankie were coming after me. So before they took him back to the glasshouse, I told him if he ever pulled a stunt like that again, I'd make sure his everloving sister got banged up even longer than he did. I thought, that'll do the trick.'

'Instead of which it just gave him another reason for wanting to sort you out.'

'Worse. I reckon he told Jude. I don't think she'd be risking everything she's got just for love of Tankie. No, she's got her own agenda here, protecting her own interests, her own life.'

'While actually you don't have anything on her at all! Great move, sir. Really clever thinking!'

'Nobody's perfect,' said Dalziel without conviction.

'Joe E. Brown. *Some Like It Hot*,' said Pascoe.

'What the fuck are you on about?' said Dalziel. 'Stand by! Here we go again.'

Once more he was a second ahead in detecting the key in the door.

This time Trotter didn't enter the room but stood in the doorway. Pascoe saw his eyes take in the name scratched on the wall above the bed. Then he was screaming, '*Prisoner!* Double mark time!'

Dalziel began running on the spot.

'Higher! Get them knees up higher!' yelled Trotter. 'You great bag of lard. We shouldn't be feeding you, we should be fasting you till you start looking like a human being instead of a blubber fucking whale! At the double, forward march. Left wheel! Keep them knees up, d'you hear me? Lef'ri'lef'ri'lef'ri' . . .'

Dalziel went out of the dairy with Trotter in close attendance. Pascoe took a tentative step towards the door, but Judith was there, the gun in her hands as steady as the grey eyes fixed on his face.

He forced himself to take another small step forward.

'Next one takes you off the edge of the world,' she said.

She had a low-pitched voice with a not displeasing huskiness. If she could hold a note, he could imagine her coming over like Bacall in *To Have and Have Not*. (Did Andy Williams *really* dub that?) He put on his Bogart lisp and said, 'Somewhere this has got to stop, you must see that. So it makes sense, the sooner the better.'

The gun barrel moved forward as slightly but as certainly as a Socratic question exposing a flaw in his argument. He gave way before it, retreating both steps he'd advanced and another besides. Bogie wasn't too proud to be scared. Remember *Key Largo*!

'If you kill me . . .' He meant to urge on her the inevitable consequences to herself, her brother, the moral health of the Nation, and the Rule of Law. Instead he heard pathos slipping into bathos as he concluded limply, '. . . I'll be dead.'

Even as he thought, 'Oh God! I didn't really say that, did I?' he saw a reaction. First she smiled . . . that was at the bathos. And then the smile faded and for the first time she blinked as if something other than blank watchfulness was trying to show itself in her eyes. Perhaps that was the pathos getting to her. Perhaps for the first time she was seeing him not just as an adjunct of the gross Dalziel but as a young man with a life still to live, wine still to drink, movies still to see, girls still to . . .

He found he was blinking tears back from his eyes. Well, it had been a hard day so far and he'd had no breakfast. Even as he fought against this weakness which he suspected unfitted him to be a policeman he found himself wondering how his complete breakdown would affect the woman, which perhaps meant he was cut out to be a cop after all.

Before he could test just how meltable she was, he heard the sound of Dalziel's footsteps with their high-pitched *lef'ri'lef'ri'lef* accompaniment. The Fat Man appeared in the cell with a pint mug in one hand and a plate piled with some kind of stew in the other. At Trotter's command he marked time at the foot of the bed. Despite all his efforts at steadiness tea slopped out of the mug at every step and gravy dripped off the edge of the plate.

'Look what you're doing to the officer's meal!' screamed Trotter. 'I've a good mind to make you lick it up, you horrible man. HALT. LEFT TURN. Give the officer his meal and apologize for the mess you've made.'

'SIR!' shouted Dalziel breathlessly. 'Here's your meal, SIR! Sorry about the mess, SIR!'

He didn't look well, thought Pascoe. Or perhaps that greyness round the mouth was his natural colouring. The eyes were lively enough, full of promissory vengeance which came across as all embracing rather than targeted.

Even if I get out of this lot, thought Pascoe, I don't get the feeling I've much of a future in Mid Yorkshire!

He dug deep for his Alec Guinness voice. Because of the thickness in his throat it came out more *Tunes of Glory* than *Bridge on the River Kwai*.

'Carry on, Mr Trotter.'

And the poor fat sod was off again, doubling back down to the kitchen presumably to get his own grub this time.

Pascoe looked speculatively at the woman. The old blankness was back. Impervious she might be to hot tears, but how would she react to hot stew in her face?

Badly, he answered himself. And in these confined quarters there wasn't much chance of ducking out of the spread of two shotgun barrels.

He took a careful sip of his tea, then set it on the floor and examined the stew. There was a spoon half submerged in its rich brownness which gave off a good appetizing smell reminding him he'd missed breakfast. While there was life, there was hunger. He began to eat. It tasted as good as it smelt and he'd almost finished by the time Dalziel returned, clutching another mug and plate.

Trotter noticed his progress and said, 'Sir! Like another helping, sir?'

He almost said yes, then he looked at Dalziel still double marking time, and thought it would mean another trip to the kitchen for the poor sod.

'No, thank you, Mr Trotter,' he said.

'Right, sir. Thank you, sir. Prisoner, HALT! Stan' atease. Next inspection in thirty minutes.'

Then he was gone. Dalziel waited till they heard the key turn in the lock before subsiding slowly onto the bed.

'You OK, sir?' said Pascoe.

The great grey head turned slowly towards him.

'What's up, lad? Worried in case I snuff it and there's nowt between you and Tankie but your fancy degree? Rest quiet. There's nothing wrong with me that a good woman and a bottle of High- land Park wouldn't put right.'

'Glad to hear it, sir. Talking of a good woman, was Mrs Dalziel expecting you to drop in at home before you went back to Wales? If so . . .'

'Forget it, lad. There is no Mrs Dalziel now.'

'I'm sorry,' said Pascoe. 'Dead?'

'No such sodding luck,' grunted the Fat Man. 'Just divorced. You married?'

'No sir.'

'Good. First thing I've heard in your favour so far. Not engaged or owt like that? Girlfriend filling her bottom drawer?'

'No sir. There was a girl at university . . .'

'Oh aye. The one got you auditioning for *An Inspector Calls*? She still hanging around?'

'No sir. Not the type who hangs around. Not the type who likes her boyfriends joining the police force either.'

'One of them? Then you're well rid of her,' growled Dalziel. 'Ee, that weren't half bad. Wouldn't like to fetch me another helping, would you?'

He'd been demolishing his stew as he talked and now he thrust the plate towards Pascoe who took it and half rose before he remembered.

'Nice to see that being an officer for five minutes hasn't spoilt your manners,' grinned Dalziel.

Angrily Pascoe threw the plate onto the bed. It skidded off the mattress, hit the stone-flagged floor and shattered.

'Clever,' said Dalziel. 'Tha knows who'll get the blame for that?'

'Why the hell aren't we talking about how to get out of here instead of exchanging dull details of our domestic lives?' demanded Pascoe. 'Everyone seems to think you're so bloody marvellous, why don't you do something to prove it?'

'Got a temper, have you?' said Dalziel not disapprovingly. 'All right. Here. Take hold of that.'

He reached down and picked up two long sharp shards of china, one of which he handed to Pascoe.

He went on. 'First chance we get, we jump 'em. You grab the lass, get a hold of her hair, stick that into her throat or her eye, any bit of her you can get at that'll do a lot of damage. Think you can manage that, lad?'

Pascoe looked at the fragment of plate and imagined sinking it into one of those pale grey eyes . . .

'I'm not sure, sir . . .' he said.

'Oh aye? So while I'm doing the business on Tankie, Jude's turning my spine into bonemeal? No thanks. We need another plan. Your turn.'

He tossed the plate shard back onto the floor and looked expectantly at the younger man.

'I don't know,' cried Pascoe. 'I meant something more like escaping . . . this isn't a prison, I mean it wasn't built to keep people in. Surely we can find a way to get out . . . ?'

'Like the Count of Monte Cristo, you mean? Now that were a good movie. Robert Doughnut, weren't it? Only they had to dig for about twenty years, didn't they? About the same amount of time you spent in school, learning fuck all. Tell you what, why don't you take the first shift, lad?'

It wasn't so much the words as the Fat Man's more-in-pain-than-in-anger expression that got to Pascoe.

He said, 'You're forgetting something. It wasn't the tunnel that got him out, it was the old sod dying and being dumped in the sea in a sack. Our only problem is going to be, where will we find a sack big enough?'

He'd gone too far. If Dalziel looked big before, now he seemed to swell monstrously like the genie let out of the bottle in *The Thief of Baghdad*.

He tried to recall how Sabu had got him back in again. By persuading him he *couldn't* get back in again!

He forced a smile and said, 'You got a temper too, sir? Maybe we're a matching pair.'

For a moment, the Fat Man trembled on the brink of nuclear fission. Then, slowly subsiding, he snarled, 'Man who can believe that should stick to directing traffic.'

His anger must have dulled his hearing for he was still on the bed when the door flew open and Trotter erupted, yelling, 'What the hell's going on here? Who broke that plate? Prisoner giving you trouble, sir?'

Dalziel was back at rigid attention, the genie well back inside.

Pascoe said, 'Accident, Mr Trotter. Prisoner rather emotional. Private interview with officer i.c. As per regulations.'

He was gabbling. He tried to change it to the sternness of reproof, decided that perhaps it wasn't such a good idea and stuck with his gabble.

Happily Trotter wasn't paying him much attention. He stepped back to the doorway, picked up a bucket of hot water his sister had set down there and said, 'Throwing food around the place, are you, Dalziel? You may look like a pig and eat like a pig but you're not going to turn this place into a sty. I want every inch of this tip scrubbed out by the time I get back, understood?'

'SIR!'

Without a glance at Pascoe, Trotter about turned and marched out.

Oh dear, thought Pascoe. Perhaps I'm being written out of the script.

Dalziel was on his knees carefully gathering up the broken pieces of plate tunelessly whistling what might have been a bosh shot at 'Pack Up Your Troubles In Your Old Kitbag' or possibly the scherzo from Beethoven's Fifth. Pascoe looked at the bucket. There was a toothbrush floating in it.

He took it out and said, 'What's this for?'

'Scrubbing the floor,' said Dalziel.

'You're joking!'

'Well, you know what they say. If you can't take a laugh you shouldn't have joined. What's up, lad? You've got that gormless college look on thy face again.'

Pascoe said slowly, 'He had this bucket ready when he came in. As if he knew about the broken plate in advance.'

'Coincidence. Good guesser,' suggested Dalziel.

'Maybe. Or maybe . . .' He stopped voicing the words but mouthed at Dalziel, '. . . he's listening!'

To his amazement Dalziel roared with laughter and applauded.

He's bluffing, thought Pascoe. The old bastard's only pretending he knew all along. How could he . . . oh shit! The wallet. He'd told Dalziel he'd dropped his wallet and a few minutes later Trotter had come in with it. Dalziel had worked it out, this fat, loutish, stupid . . . It was the animal cunning thing, of course. OK, so he'd worked it out, but he didn't have that wider mental scope which might have enabled him to *use* his knowledge. Whereas if he, Peter Pascoe, BA, had realized, he would have . . . what? He tried to think of some way of utilizing the situation.

He looked at Dalziel who was now down on his knees methodically scrubbing the floor with the toothbrush.

Pascoe said, 'Sir . . .'

'Aye?' prompted the Fat Man, but Pascoe was finding speech problematical. Suppose he said . . . ? But if he said . . . ?

Dalziel said, 'Do you reckon the scientists in them vivisectionist places pay much heed to the squeaking of the rats?'

Pascoe whispered, 'You think he's going to kill us then?'

'Speak up, lad. Can't hear you.'

'Do you think he's going to kill us?' shouted Pascoe.

'Depends. He is doolally, even Tankie couldn't deny that. But is he so far gone that killing a man he hates is worth spending the rest of his life banged up for? And if he thinks it is, then he may decide to chuck you in for good measure, that's what you really want to know, isn't it?'

'But why kill me? I've done nothing?'

He knew he sounded plaintive, but if Tankie *were* listening, then perhaps this was a plea for his life and he wasn't going to let embarrassment stand in the way.

'Well,' said Dalziel judiciously, 'he might do it 'cos he thinks you're one of my boys, an extension of me so to speak. If he's not cottoned on how far from the truth that is, let me set him right. I've never seen you in my life afore today, right? You've been transferred into the squad behind my back without my agreement, and having had the pleasure of seeing you in action this last couple of hours, I think I can fairly promise if I do come out of this alive to make it my life's work to get you sent back to whatever kindergarten you escaped from! No offence intended.'

'None taken,' said Pascoe. 'In the same spirit of openness, may I say that I'd rather serve as an underground maintenance man in a sewage works than continue in your employ, sir.'

'Glad we've got all that cleared up,' said Dalziel. 'On the other hand if Tankie thinks that, just because he's topped me, he's got to top you as well to give him a chance of getting away with it, well, he really has flipped it. He's in the frame already. Fingerprints all over my car. He wasn't wearing gloves, was he? And God knows who saw him around the place. Then they'll find this cottage eventually. Lot depends on how clever Jude was. I reckon she'd have to set it up. Probably didn't want to, all she's got to lose. But she owes Tankie, 'cos without him things 'ud've been even worse for her and her mum all them years. And he's her twin.

And the bother he got into with the army was mainly because of his family. So, did she find this hole through an ad or go through an agent? Wieldy told me that he were told they'd gone off on a trip. Sooner or later they'll trace t'others. Could take days. Or it could be they've done it already and the army's crawling around the bushes outside.'

Did he really believe that? wondered Pascoe. Of course not, else he wouldn't be saying it. Would he?

'Mind moving your feet?' said the Fat Man. 'I need to scrub under them. By the by, here's a tip. If the tear gas comes in, stick your head in this bucket of water.'

'That will help with the gas?' asked Pascoe.

'Nay, it's just that the sharpshooters have been taught not to blast off at a man with his head in a bucket!'

He bellowed a laugh, and Pascoe thought disgustedly, he's a total clown. Except that the eyes regarding him were shrewd and almost sympathetic.

'No use feeling sorry for yourself, lad,' said Dalziel. 'Like my old ma always used to say, there's plenty worse off than you.'

'Name one.'

'That poor lass Judith for a start,' said Dalziel. 'Tankie's got nowt to lose except his freedom, and to tell truth, I reckon that after all this time, the notion of being free scares the shit out of him. But Judith's got a life to go back to. OK she'd get her knuckles rapped for helping him, but no one's really going to blame her for running scared of a loonie like Tankie and jumping when he says jump! Look at me. I'm jumping aren't I? And I've not got any kids or loved ones he can threaten. We snuff it, but, and Jude can say goodbye to all that. Cleft stick, poor cow. How about you, Sonny Jim? You got anyone who'll miss you, apart from the *Inspector Calls* lass?'

'I told you, she's history,' said Pascoe shortly. 'When I told her I wanted to be a cop, she and her mates started singing that song from *Going My Way* whenever I came into the bar. The one with the line: *or would you rather be a pig?*'

'Bing Crosby,' said the Fat Man. He started to sing in a booming baritone, '*Would you like to swing on a star? Carry moonbeams home in a jar?* Daft bloody words. Daft bloody woman. You're well shut of her. How about family? Is your mam really dead?'

'No, I'm glad to say. Nor my father. And I've got two elder sisters, so there's still an active family unit in existence.'

'Oh aye? Sounds right cosy. I bet you have active family unit reunions at Christmas and birthdays and such,' sneered Dalziel.

The old bastard certainly had a nose for sniffing out trouble, thought Pascoe, feeling a great longing to launch the toe of his shoe at the kneeling man's buttocks.

I'd probably break my leg, he thought.

He said, 'I think my private life is none of your business, just as yours is none of mine. As long as we do the job we're paid for . . .'

Dalziel paused in his scrubbing and looked up at him, the great mouth rounding in big-close-up astonishment.

'*We*?' he said. 'As in you and me? In the same word? Like we were doing the same job? Now listen, sunshine, you'd better get yourself disenchanted. Man who can believe we've got owt in common except two bollocks and a bunghole, and I'm not sure about you, could end up owning a lot of clapped-out used cars.'

'Oh you're right, sir,' said Pascoe angrily. 'I'm so sorry. I'd heard a lot about you and I now see I was wrong not to believe every incredible word. From the moment I heard you this morning allegedly giving evidence on behalf of that poor woman, I knew the last thing I wanted was to be tarred with your brush. Sir!'

'No need to get personal,' said Dalziel looking hurt. 'What were wrong with my evidence anyway?'

'Wrong? You were the main prosecution witness . . .'

'No, lad. That were the woman,' corrected Dalziel gently.

'Yes, and just because she was a prostitute and you felt there was little chance of a conviction, you'd clearly decided the whole thing was a waste of time!'

'Aye, well, you're half right, I'll give you that,'

Dalziel replied disconcertingly. 'That's exactly the line yon donkey-pizzle, Martineau, was taking. So I just made sure the jury got a wink and a nod that this weren't no jolly punter willing to pay for a quick bang, but a career sex offender who won't be stopped till it's lopped off!'

'Oh, yes? Easy to say that now,' sneered Pascoe.

'Nay, lad. Easier not to say it at all and I don't know why I bothered,' sighed Dalziel. 'What's a sprog daft enough to correct a magistrate's jokes know about giving evidence?'

Pascoe digested this then exploded, 'So you've been spying on me as well!'

'I went into a public court to see one of my junior officers giving evidence, yes. Bet you thought you were doing all right, too, eh?'

'Yes, as a matter of fact, I did. Damn sight better than you anyway,' said Pascoe who was almost beginning to enjoy the crackling heat of his burning bridges.

'Oh aye? Tell you what. Ten bob says my scrote got sent down, your pair walked free.'

Pascoe did a mental double-take. Against volition, his jaw, as craggily set as Spencer Tracy's in the expectation of moral showdown, dropped. He must have missed something. Otherwise how come he'd moved from career-ending confrontation to settling matters with a friendly bet like two chaps in a pub?

He looked at the Fat Man with growing suspicion. Could it possibly be that this cop, so obviously the archetypical bruiser who got results by kicking down doors and beating out questions in Morse code on a suspect's head, was in fact jerking him around with *words*? No! Reason wouldn't admit it . . . or was it pride that wouldn't admit it? He tried to bring to mind the scene in the court . . . the jury laughing . . . Martineau furious . . . was that the key . . . ? Should he have listened more carefully . . . ?

Dalziel straightened up and broke wind.

'Better out than in,' he said. 'So, is it a bet?'

'I'd need odds,' said Pascoe. 'There's two of mine.'

'You cheeky sod. All right. Ten bob to a quid. How's that?'

'Done,' said Pascoe.

'Grand. And I reckon this is done too.'

He pushed himself to his feet rather creakingly and massaged his knees. Then he looked at his watch and said, 'I'll never make it back to Taff-land in time for the kick-off now. Not to worry. I daresay I'll see a bit too much of yon little bugger over the next ten years or so. Here, Tankie's taking his time about the next inspection, isn't he?'

'I'm not complaining,' said Pascoe.

'Well, you bloody well should be. Officer present, prisoner ready for inspection, and the RSM absent from parade? It's not bloody on! Excuse me, SIR!'

And Pascoe, who was getting used to finding himself tumbling in zero gravity every time he began to feel something like firm ground beneath his feet, was hardly surprised to be pushed aside as the Fat Man began to beat a thunderous rhythm on the door accompanied by a raucous bellow of, 'Come on, Tankie, let's be having you. Plenty of time to sit around playing with yourself when this lot's over. Charley, Charley, get out of bed! Charley, Charley . . .'

Pascoe got well clear of the door but this time instead of being flung violently against the wall, it swung slowly open. Trotter stood there, the sawn-off shotgun at the high port. His face was so impassive, it just needed a cheroot to get him auditioned for a spaghetti western.

He didn't look like he'd come to play at inspections.

'This do you then?' said Dalziel cheerfully, picking up the bucket. 'The floor's so clean you could eat your dinner off it. Shan't be needing this any more.'

And in an act too suicidal for Pascoe to find an appropriate reaction, the Fat Man hurled the water in Trotter's face.

It wasn't the preliminary to an escape attempt. Dalziel just stood there roaring with laughter. Nor did Trotter react with any explosive show of anger. Instead, the water dripping down his face, he slowly and deliberately brought the gun barrel to bear on Dalziel's chest.

'Nay, Tankie, fair do's,' protested the Fat Man. 'When you chucked your bucket in yon colour sergeant's face, he didn't shoot you, did he? And there were a lot worse than water in it! Mind you, I'm not saying he didn't feel like it, but he kept control.'

'I'm not a bloody colour sergeant,' grated Trotter.

'That's right. And I'm not a squaddy and this ain't the glasshouse. So where does that get us? You want to prove that if I had to put up with what you had to put up with, I'd crack like a Boxing Day wishbone. Well, wish away, lad, but it's not going to come true. Tha's not got the time and tha's not got the talent. So where do we go from here?'

Only one place! Pascoe's fears told him. But fear left just sufficient space for another voice which asked, why is Dalziel doing this? Why the change of tactics? And if there is a game, why the hell couldn't the big, fat, arrogant bastard let me in on it? Because he thinks I'm useless? Because he thinks he's God?

Because, came a tiny voice from somewhere deeper than reason, because he knew from the start that everything we said was overheard by Trotter.

Could it really be that this Quasimodo, this Incredible Hulk, this Creature From The Black Lagoon had been carefully orchestrating everything he said? Oh, that would be a trick worth knowing, even if it took a lifetime to learn. Did he have a lifetime? He was beginning to hope again. But perhaps it was all just a clutching at straws. His mind was racing through the Fat Man's inconsequential ramblings . . . his bad jokes . . . desperately seeking the small man in the booth who was working the Great Oz's lips . . .

'Tell you what, Tankie,' said Dalziel. 'Why don't you chuck it in? Leave us locked up and take off. I'll not chase you, believe me. Less I see of you in future the better. You can settle down somewhere, forget the past. Jude too. Past's dead and buried. Like your dad. Finished and forgotten, all debts paid. No names, no pack drill. You can both have a future. You wherever you go. And Jude back home with her man and her kiddie . . .'

And at last Pascoe saw it, clear as the hair in Dalziel's nose. All those casual references to Judith's settled life . . . Tankie had known nothing of this! The poor bastard really had believed that during all his time behind bars, his twin had been shut away too in some empathic fastness of the heart and mind, living only for his release, their reunion.

Dalziel had worked this out, guessed that Jude's co-operation wasn't just based on geminate love, or even fear that the Fat Man could tie her in to her father's death, but the much greater fear that if Tankie knew the truth, he might divert some or all of these pent-up energies from destruction of Dalziel to destruction of her precious new life.

So why hadn't the Fat Man just spilled the beans straight off?

Because Tankie would probably have killed the

messenger! This way, by letting him work it out for himself . . .

It was all a question of timing, of working out when the hints had finally worked. And they had worked. The evidence was there in the woman's face, floating in the shadows over her brother's shoulder. One cheek pale as a winter sky, the other flushed like a summer dawn.

The bastard had hit her. And then Dalziel had summoned him. Why?

So he could learn about the child, of course!

This revelation the Fat Man had kept for now, for face to face, guessing that Jude would keep hidden to the end what she valued most, even in face of – especially in face of! – Tankie's rage. For here was the clincher. A social life, a job, even a fellow, after the first explosion, these could be rationalized away. But a child . . .

Even Tankie would know this meant he was relegated to at least second place forever.

He was looking at her now, seeking confirmation in those eyes which so weirdly mirrored his own.

Pascoe glanced at Dalziel hoping for some sign of how he wanted to play this. Was the idea to take the chance offered by this moment of distraction and jump the Trotters? Or was he relying on the revelation having some softening effect on Tankie, making him realize that any further development of his crazy vengeance plan would not only destroy himself and his sister, but her child too?

He'd have betted on violence, but once again he

saw he was wrong. The Fat Man was putting his money on psychology, turning now to the locker and taking his suit out.

'I'll be glad to get back into this,' he said. 'Wearing that stuff's like wiping your bum with sandpaper. Like to avert your eyes, Jude? Or do you reckon, seen one, you've seen 'em all?'

He pushed his fatigue trousers down as he spoke. And Pascoe, watching Trotter's face in profile, saw that for all his jungle cunning, the Fat Man had miscalculated.

Perhaps it was Dalziel's coarseness. Or perhaps it was the confirmation in his sister's expression of all that she'd kept from him, and why she'd kept it, and the difference it must make to their relationship for evermore.

Or perhaps it was simply that if fear of your reputation as a wild beast is the nearest you've had to respect in a waste of years, then a wild beast's response is the only option you ever have.

Reasons didn't matter. Nothing mattered except that he was swinging the gun round to blow the Fat Man away.

As in the climactic shoot-out in *The Wild Bunch*, everything slowed down. Dalziel like a *Carry-On farceur* was immobilized with his trousers round his ankles. Pascoe didn't have time to pick a role. His body was launching itself through the air towards the Last National Service Man leaving his mind some way back, wondering why the hell he should *give* a damn about saving the Fat Man for posterity.

Probably posterity would still have been spared this Grecian gift if Judith hadn't got in on the act.

No doubt about her motives. Where she had imagined her brother's crazy game could lead was never clearly established. Later she claimed that the mental intimidation from her dominant twin, plus the trauma of childhood abuse, not forgetting her fear for her own child, had combined to bring her to this point almost without any conscious thought. Now all she saw was that if the Fat Man were blown away, with him went everything in her life that made any sense of it.

She jumped on her brother's back, flinging both arms round his neck and wrapping her legs around his body in a grip as sexual as a Freudian could have desired as she tried to topple him backwards. He staggered and twisted. The gun wavered away from the overhang of Dalziel's belly, and Pascoe grabbed the barrel and dragged it even further round.

Perhaps Trotter deliberately squeezed the trigger, though later, naturally, he denied it. Perhaps it was a finger-jerk reaction caused by the shock of his sister's assault. Or perhaps Pascoe himself, by pulling on the barrel, literally triggered the explosion.

Whoever or whatever, it went off.

There was no pain, just a sense of some tremendous change in his relation with the universe. Then came a couple of seconds' out-of-body experience, in which he hovered somewhere around the single light bulb, watching Dalziel step out of his trousers, advance three paces across the room and deal Trotter a blow on the temple which felled him like a blasted pylon. As he hit the ground, the whole room dissolved under a tidal wave of white light which bore Peter Pascoe out through the cottage roof and carried him at breakneck speed towards the boundary of the universe.

Later he claimed never to have lost consciousness or even the power of rational thought. For a moment, or a millennium, he even had hopes of passing through a *2001* type stargate and ending up in a nice hotel room. But gradually the white light faded and the speed diminished till finally he was simply tumbling slowly through space.

Far below he spotted the twin orbs of the earth and its circling moon. He recalled in childhood his mother trying to get him to see the man in the latter, but he'd never managed it. Now however he could see his features quite clearly in the broad bright orb, and it came as no surprise how closely they resembled those of Andy Dalziel.

The mouth was opening and shutting as if the Fat Man had something to say. Might even be worth hearing, admitted Pascoe, who was not afraid to learn from experience.

He grabbed a passing star, swung himself into a comfortable position along one of its radials, and settled down to listen.

*　　*　　*

'Think he'll make it, Wieldy?'

'They say there's no reason why not, sir.'

'Well, he better bloody had.'

'Yes sir. Any particular reason, apart from general humanity, sir?'

'He owes me ten bob, that particular enough for you?'

'Oh yes. What'll you do with him if he does make it?'

'Likely I'll keep him. It'll be a challenge.'

'And if he doesn't want to be kept?'

'Nay, Wieldy, you don't imagine I want anybody working for me who's daft enough to want to work for me, do you? A scared cop is a good cop, as long as it don't stop him thinking. And this bugger kept on thinking.'

'Yes, sir. I think he'll do a lot of that. But I shouldn't bank on him staying scared forever.'

'No? Mebbe not. But there's one bugger who should be running scared for the rest of his life. That's the stupid sod who told Tankie where to find me!'

'Sorry, sir?'

'I asked Tankie when he woke up how come he knew I'd be down at the courts. He said he rang the station and asked to speak to me, and some stupid bastard told him I was away for a while, but I'd be back that morning to give evidence. Can you credit it, Wieldy? No idea who he were speaking to, and this bumbrain gives chapter and verse where I can be found!'

Peter Pascoe, who'd been thinking he might try

dropping off his star onto the earth next time it rolled past, decided that maybe he'd give it another couple of whirls.

Andy Dalziel said, 'I could murder a cup of tea, Wieldy. And a bun if you can find one.'

The door opened and shut. The Fat Man leaned over the bed and glowered into Pascoe's pale face.

'Anyone at home?' he asked. 'If there is, here's the deal. It'll be grapes and gruel for a bit, then it'll be hard bloody graft for evermore. 'Cos I'm going to make a man out of you, my son. You're going to be the very last National Service Man. Only it's no soft two-year stint for you. Serve with me and you're in for the bloody duration. I'll badger you, and I'll bully you, and I'll bugger you about something rotten. But I'll not take advantage of you or make a dickhead out of you or fob you off with a load of lies. And when I've driven that college crap out of your head, then we'll find out what you're really made of. You may never amount to much as a cop, but by God, you'll learn to jump when I say jump, and that's something. Aye lad, by the time I'm done, if I tell you to fetch me the moon, you'll take off like a whippet and not come back till you've got it in your gob . . . what's that you say?'

Pascoe's lips had moved. The Fat Man stooped closer to catch the softly breathed words.

'. . . let's not ask for the moon . . . I'd rather swing on a star . . .'

'Eh?' said Dalziel.

The eyes snapped open, the words came loud and clear.

'Bette Davis. *Now Voyager*. Almost.'

And for the first time in his life, Andrew Dalziel wondered if he might be biting off more than even his great cetacean jaws could manage to chew.

On Beulah Height

Reginald Hill

They moved everyone out of Dendale that long hot summer fifteen years ago. They needed a new reservoir and an old community seemed a cheap price to pay. They even dug up the dead and moved them too.

But four inhabitants of the valley they couldn't move, for no one knew where they were. Three little girls had gone missing, and the prime suspect in their disappearance, Benny Lightfoot.

This was Andy Dalziel's worst case and now fifteen years on he looks set to relive it. It's another long hot summer. A child goes missing in the next valley, and old fears resurface as someone sprays the deadly message on the walls of Danby: BENNY'S BACK!

Music and myth mingle as the Mid-Yorkshire team delve into their pasts and into their own reserves of experience and endurance in search of answers which threaten to bring more pain than they resolve.

'All Reginald Hill's novels are brilliantly written, but he has excelled himself here: and has, too, put together an intricate narrative with the complex ingenuity of a watchmaker'
                                T. J. BINYON, *Evening Standard*

ISBN-13: 978-0-00-649000-5

Under World

Reginald Hill

When young Tracey Pedley went brambling in the woods around Burrthorpe and vanished, the close-knit mining community had its own ideas about what happened, and people wondered about the last man to see her alive and his fatal plunge into a disused mine shaft.

Returning to a town he left in anger, Colin Farr's home-coming is fraught with anguish, but a university course brings him into contact with Ellie Pascoe – and her husband Peter's life will never be the same again.

Meanwhile, Andy Dalziel mutters imprecations on the sidelines, until a murder in Burrthorpe mine forces him to take action that brings him into contact with a hostile and frightened community . . .

'A scintillating performance that rattles some real bones of social anger'   *Observer*

ISBN-13: 978-0-586-20452-8

Bones and Silence
Reginald Hill

When Detective Superintendent Andrew Dalziel witnesses a bizarre murder across the street from his own back garden, he is quite sure who the culprit is. After all, he's got to believe what he sees with his own eyes. But what exactly does he see? And is he mistaken?

Dalziel senses the doubters around him, which only strengthens his resolve, and to make matters worse, he's being pestered by an anonymous letter writer threatening suicide.

Meanwhile, the effervescent Eileen Chung is directing the Mystery Plays for the local theatre group. And who does she have in mind to play God? None other than the Super himself. He shouldn't have too much difficulty acting the part.

'Reginald Hill is on stunning form . . . the climax is devastating'
The Times

ISBN-13: 978-0-586-21128-1

The Wood Beyond
Reginald Hill

A ravaged, cratered wood, a man in uniform long dead –
this is not a World War One battlefield, but Wanwood
House, a pharmaceutical research centre.

Away to the south, Peter Pascoe is attending his grandmother's funeral, and scattering her ashes leads him too
into war-ravaged woods in search of his great-grandfather
who fought and died in the Passchendaele campaign.

Seeing the wood for the trees is a problem for Andy Dalziel
and Edgar Wield, the latter in his investigation into the
bones found at Wanwood, and the former in his involve-
ment with an animal rights activist, despite her possible
complicity in a murderous assault and her appalling taste
in whisky.

'This is as good as the English detective novel gets' *GQ*

'Hill's wit is the constant, ironic foil to his vision, and to
call this a mere crime novel is to say Everest is a nice little
hill' *Mail on Sunday*

ISBN-13: 978-0-00-647994-9

Good Morning, Midnight
Reginald Hill

Like father like son, but heredity seems to have gone a gene too far when Pal Maciver's suicide in a locked room exactly mirrors that of his father ten years earlier.

In each case, accusing fingers point towards Pal's step-mother, the beautiful, enigmatic Kay Kafka. But she turns out to have a formidable champion in Mid-Yorkshire's own super-heavyweight, Detective Superintendent Andrew Dalziel.

Gradually, it becomes clear that the fall-out from Pal's suicide spreads far beyond Yorkshire. To London, to America. Even to Iraq. But the emotional epicentre is firmly placed here in Mid-Yorkshire, where Pascoe comes to learn that for some people the heart, too, is a locked room – and in there, it is always midnight.

'Unfolds compellingly and displays all his familiar intelligence and wit. *Good Morning, Midnight* shows Hill on top form'
Sunday Times

'The writing is brilliant, witty and erudite…as enjoyable as anything Reginald Hill has ever produced'
Evening Standard

'Hill's book will keep you reading far beyond the midnight hour'
Sunday Express

ISBN-13: 978-0-00-712343-8

The Stranger House
Reginald Hill

They came to The Stranger House. And death followed close behind.

For over 500 years, the Stranger House has stood in the village of Illthwaite, offering refuge to all manner of travellers. People like Sam Flood, a brilliant young Australian mathematician. And Miguel Madero, a Spanish historian who sees ghosts.

Sam is an experienced young woman, Miguel a 26-year-old virgin. But both want to dig up bits of the past that some people would rather keep buried.

As they uncover intertwining tales of murder, betrayal and love, they must put aside their differences in order to uncover the dark mysteries at the heart of this ancient place...

'Grim, gory, fascinating, enraging and entertaining'
Independent

'A mystery novel but far more than that. It's gripping... Hill is wonderful'
The Times

'You're enthralled by the cunning of the plotting... great'
Observer

ISBN-13: 978-0-00-719483-4

Arms and the Women
Reginald Hill

When Ellie Pascoe finds herself under threat, the men in her life assume it's because she's married to a cop. But while they trawl after shoals of red herrings, Ellie is blasted off course with a motley crew of women on a voyage of discovery.

Irish arms, Colombian drugs, and men who will stop at nothing create a tidal wave which threatens to sweep her away. She heads out of town in search of haven, but instead finds herself at the very edge of the storm in a remote clifftop house undermined by the sea.

Fat Andy eventually smells a Security Service rat and comes steaming to the rescue, but for once it's too little, too late. Ellie's on her own (apart from her monstrous regiment of women) and must reach deep down into her reserves to find the strength to survive.

'Luminously written, thrilling in the best old-fashioned sense of the word'
Daily Mail

ISBN-13: 978-0-00-651287-5